Natalie Smiles

Life After Lupus

By: Chiemeri Osemele

In loving Memory of Natalie McNally. Whose smile is on our hearts and minds, forever.

1

I'm Natalie!

"I think ice cream trucks were made by Santa," said a girl named Natalie

"What nooooo. Santa doesn't make ice cream Natalie," said a girl named Chichi,

"Then who does?" said Natalie.

"I don't know. A big factory, I guess. Or the ice cream man in the truck," Chichi replied.

Hi! My name is Natalie, and that was me and my best friend Chichi having an important conversation about ice cream. Chichi is Nigerian. Her full name is beautiful but hard for some to say, so we all just call her Chichi. I remember her telling me her full name means, "God has won" or something like that. Which I thought was really cool. I don't know what my name means, but I like it! I think it fits me. Anyway, that was a long time ago but I remember it always. It was when I stayed in suburbs with my parents.

Right now, I live with the angels and Jesus in heaven. Jesus loves me so much and he loves you too. Sometimes I miss home but being here makes me happy too.

I'm sure you are wondering why I live in heaven and how I got here. Don't worry I'm very very safe and so happy! I'm going to tell you my story and how I got to live with Jesus now.

I hope you are ready because it's exciting, fun, and sometimes sad, and even silly. Me and my best friend Chichi, we goof around a lot....

So, my home was in a small town in a big city. It had a funny name, which was Hollow Hearth. My house was beautiful. I had my own room; my own toys like Mr. Pooh bear and My Beanie Babies; I had some nice clothes in all my favorite colors, and nice shoes too.

I went to school five days a week and although I liked it there; I hated homework. My friend Chichi went to my school too. We had lots of other friends, but we were BFFs. Sometimes we would walk home after school and Chichi and I would chase the butterflies near a small garden in the park. I caught one once in a jar. It had such beautiful colors.

"I wish I was a butterfly," I said.

"Me too. Then we would fly all over Hollow Hearth and see the skies and maybe chase that mean girl in class." Chichi said, and we both laughed and laughed.

We opened the jar, and the butterfly came out. It flew around our heads before flying away. I think it said goodbye.

During the weekend our parents would go on a picnic or to a fun place and take us with them. My parents were friends with Chichi's parents. In fact, my Mommy was BFFs with Chichi's Mommy. I always knew we were meant to be friends forever. They let us run off to play and come right back before they got worried. I was very happy and so was everyone. But when I got sick, many people became sad.

2

Monday- My best day of the school week.

I loved Mondays. I had my classes in school on Mondays and dancing class for an hour after school. It was always so exciting.

"Natalie, get your bag pack you are going to be late for school," shouted Daddy. My Daddy was my second BFF. I wanted to be just like him when I grew up. He was more fun than all my dolls and smart too. He worked in a big office and loved oldies Music, so I did too! Blondie, The Beach Boys, The Bangles, I loved all of it and would sing the songs to ChiChi who thought it was cool, cause her Mommy and Daddy listened to a different kind of Oldies. Pointer Sisters, Donna Summer, Bob Marley, stuff like that. Daddy always said he and Mommy made a great team and that's why he loves her.

"Daddy, I think I forgot my new socks," I said as I rushed down from the car and back into the house again.

"What do you need your new socks for?" Daddy asked,

"I want to show Chichi. She has to get them too, so we can have matching socks for our talent show in school." I said as I climbed into the backseat.

I arrived at school just in time. I felt tired. Probably because I ran all around the house this morning I thought. So I walked a bit slow to class. My English teacher Mrs. Goldapp hated children walking in late. She hardly smiled, but she was such a great teacher. She lowered her glasses as I walked in a few seconds late to my seat.

"Sorry Mrs. Goldapp," I said. Someone poked my arm from the side. It was Chichi. We smiled at each other.

"Are you okay? You look weird?" she whispered.

"I feel so tired. I brought the socks." I whispered back as I smiled even more.

Mrs. Goldapp hit her ruler on the board and started calling out words for us to repeat.

I was tired the whole school day. Chichi kept wondering what was wrong because I loved Mondays. I didn't know. Maybe I needed to sleep more like Mommy says I thought. I always loved to read storybooks after my parents kiss me goodnight. Mommy told me kids need at least eight hours of sleep every night.

When the school closed, we ran straight to dance class which was also in the school building. The mean girl, Berta was part of our dance class. I didn't like her and neither did Chichi because she was so mean to everyone. She sometimes bullied other kids.

Our dance teacher was a nice lady. She smiled a lot like me and loved to dress in cartoon character outfits. Today she wore a Spongebob shirt. I thought it was so cute.

We started dancing and showing the steps we learned last week. I missed a few but our teacher said I did well. Suddenly, her phone rang.

"Okay. Rest a little. I will be right back." She said as she went to a corner to talk to her phone.

"Your shirt looks dumb," Berta said to another kid.

"Mine is prettier. Your glove looks fine. I should try it on." Berta continued as she tried to force the gloves from the kid.

"Leave her alone Berta. Those are not yours and you should say please." I said.

"They are not your gloves Natalie," Berta screamed at me.

"Don't shout at her," Chichi said.

Berta kept trying to take the gloves from the other kid who was much smaller than her. It was awful. So, I tried to separate them. Then I fell.

"Natalie! What is wrong with you Berta?" Chichi screamed as she rushed to me.

"Are you okay? Come on get up" she continued. But I couldn't get up. I was so tired. Just then, our teacher came over. She saw me on the floor.

"What is going on here girls? Natalie, are you okay? You are burning up. Are you unwell?" she asked as she touched my forehead and neck.

I was too tired to answer her. So she scooped me up and my eyelids closed. I slept and dreamt of a Krusty Krab adventure with Spongebob.

3

Too Tired!

I remember little of what happened after the dance class. I slept for the rest of the day. I didn't go to school on Tuesday either because my Mommy said I had to stay home and rest. She kept checking my temperature. I only felt tired, but I guess I had a fever because Mommy said so. She brought some drugs which I hated. They tasted yucky. But I took them anyway.

I didn't go back to school until the next week. I was happy it was Monday again.

"Natalie, look, I got the matching socks," said Chichi as we ate our lunch. We giggled and showed each other our feet.

Then I heard some boys in our class talking about the talent show. Oh no! I had forgotten about the talent show; I thought.

"Chichi, the talent show! We didn't practice." I said.

"You had a fever. We can still practice. Remember, you are super talented, and I already learned my song." Chichi explained.

We had decided to do a singing performance where I would play the flute the way my cousin taught me during the summer break. Chichi had a beautiful voice. I always thought she sounded like a Disney princess. So, it was right for her to sing wearing a large shiny gown.

We wanted to win. This was our first talent show.

After school, Chichi and I walked home together. She sang her song, and it was great. I practiced the flute too at home. That sounded great too, just some parts I needed more practice.

I heard my Mommy and Daddy talking in the kitchen. My Mommy's voice was sad. So I went to listen.

"I don't know. The tests are not done yet. I don't like this at all." Mommy said

"It will be okay. She will be okay." Daddy said as he hugged Mommy. I wondered what happened. I wanted to ask Mommy not to be sad, but I was too tired. So I went back to my room to sleep a little.

I felt sick for the rest of the week. And the week after that. Sometimes I had a fever and Mommy would get worried. Her hands sometimes shook when she rubbed my head. I smiled. I wanted her to be happy.

Soon it was time for our talent show. I was very excited. Chichi's Mommy bought her a new dress. It was pink, and it was shiny. I wore a dress too and carried my flute. Everyone we knew came to watch the talent show. There were other kids and their parents. Our teachers and Principal Walsh were also there.

Some of us stayed behind the big curtain. When you heard your name then you could climb the big stage. Berta was with us. She and her mean friends wore matching ballerina clothes. They were going to dance. She laughed at the kids who made mistakes on the stage. I was too tired to stop her.

"Natalie and Chichi!" It was time, we heard our names.

"Ready?" I smiled at Chichi and held her hands. We were going to win and show Berta.

"Yea," she replied.

We walked to the big stage. I didn't know there were so many people. Chichi took the microphone but her voice was so small.

"Hi… we are going to do a song," she said

We smiled and bowed. Chichi started singing. She had to sing a little before I played. I waited then I put the flute on my lip. Something bad happened. I couldn't play it very well. My fingers won't move properly. I tried, but it was so much work. Everyone was waiting. Chichi had to keep singing as she looked at me. I could tell she was confused. This was not what we rehearsed. I couldn't play. I stopped trying. I looked at the crowd and saw my Mommy; she had that worry in her eyes again.

I felt bad and embarrassed. Chichi finished singing without me and then we bowed to leave the stage. But I cried and ran away to find my parents.

"What happened baby, don't cry, don't cry," my Mommy said as she hugged me.

"My fingers won't move. They hurt. They hurt" I cried and then my Mommy started crying too.

"It's okay, baby. I know. It's okay." She said.

We went home. I had a fever again. This time Mommy took me with her to the hospital. I loved going to Mommy's hospital where she worked, but only to visit and play doctor sometimes with Bree my doll.

I didn't like this visit though because I was sick and there was another doctor who kept checking me.

He said he was going to find out what was wrong with me. He gave me a candy, so I tried to be strong as they squeezed my arm and put a thermometer in my mouth. I slept there too.

I went home and Mommy and Daddy kept whispering around the house. Then, one day Mommy came home early. Daddy was helping me guide my fingers to write my homework. They went into their room and I hopped down from my bed to see.

My Mommy gave Daddy a paper, and she started crying.

"My baby has lupus. What are we going to do?"

My Daddy looked as sad as Mommy for the first time. He hugged her and they sat there. That was the first time I heard about lupus. This is where my story changes. I was no longer a regular kid. I had a disease called lupus. But don't worry, I was still unique.

4

That Lupus Word

"Mommy, what is lupus," I asked in my small sweet kid voice as I passed the salt and peppers in the kitchen. I didn't go to school all week again and it was boring. I wanted to play with my friends and see my teachers. I don't think Mommy liked my question because she was so surprised.

I didn't know what to say, so I was quiet and stared at the salt bottle. Mommy let out a loud sigh.

"Come on baby, it's time for an important talk with my favorite daughter!" she said,

"I'm your only daughter," I said smiling, "wait what about dinner. I'm hungry."

"Okay, let's eat first," Mommy said.

We had dinner in the living room together. We didn't use the dining area. We watched a really funny movie. After dinner, Mommy and Daddy came into my room. They told me a lot of things about lupus. Pay attention now, because I'm going to tell you too.

"Baby lupus is a disease. It means you are sick." Daddy started,

"You mean like the flu?" I asked,

"Yes, like the flu. But lupus is different. It is kind of where your body fights itself. Like the little cells in your body fight each other. Sometimes they hurt your bones or your brain, or even your heart." Mommy explained,

"But why, I didn't do anything wrong," and my eyes clouded with tears,

"Having lupus doesn't mean you did something wrong." She said.

"Do my friends have lupus?" I asked again,

"No baby. They don't," my Daddy said,

"But I do and it hurts."

"Yes, baby. Lupus makes your body hurt sometimes. It also makes you tired. But don't worry baby. You will take medicines to feel better. But you have to take them on-time." My mother said.

"Okay," I said.

"No matter what happens, we love you, baby. Always tell us how you feel. You can go to school too and do anything you always loved to do" my Daddy said.

I sniffed and wiped my teary eyes. I smiled, and I hugged my parents. They hugged me too, tight. When I slept, I dreamt of loopy lupus and I was a superhero. I took lupus with me to save my friends from the bad guys. I smiled in my sleep.

Even though I had lupus, I was still a cool kid.

I started going to school again and all my friends were glad to see me. Chichi wasn't mad about the talent show. We didn't win. Berta and her mean friends won the talent show. My friends were great and understood that I now had special needs even when I looked fine on the outside.

I was tired some of the time in school, but my teachers were nice to me. I did my best. Sometimes my fingers hurt and I felt lonely because everyone else was fine. I didn't like lupus. I really wished it would go away. But I had to get used to loopy lupus. So, I did my best. I went to the hospital more and took my medications right. Maybe soon loopy lupus would be gone.

"Mommy!" I screamed from the bathroom one morning. I woke up and there was a butterfly shape on my face. It was red.

"Oh, dear," my Mommy said. She helped me have my bathe and took me to the hospital again. Dr. Chin gave me more candy and kept checking the butterfly-shaped red rash on my face. He was a rheumatologist. Pronounce it like this, roo-muh-tol-uh-jist.

My Mommy said a rheumatologist is a doctor who can treat lupus and many diseases like lupus. Dr. Chin told me the butterfly-shaped red rash was because of lupus. He said not to worry and so did Mommy. I believed my Mommy and Dr. Chin; I smiled all the way home. But in school, some kids laughed at the butterfly on my face. Some wouldn't play with me. But I still had Chichi and many other nice friends.

I was sad that day. I was sad during break and on the way home. I didn't talk to anyone. Chichi hugged me tightly after school and tried to make me laugh. I only smiled a little.

I didn't want to go to school anymore, but Daddy said I was a tough girl and tough girls don't stop going to school.

I tried to believe him and walked quietly into my school the next day. I sat at my table and looked down. I took out my pen to draw a happy cat face. Then someone poked me from the side. It was Chichi but a different Chichi.

"Surprise!" she shouted smiling,

"Why is there a butterfly on your face," I asked.

"So we can look the same. We are BFFs remember" Chichi said, and we laughed. I wasn't sad anymore. Chichi had drawn a butterfly on her face to look like me. She was a big kid and no one would laugh at us now. I loved Chichi, she was my best friend in the whole round world. We drew on our dolls too. So now we all had a butterfly on our faces.

Mommy bought me several soft and warm caps. I had so many colors, so I always wore one. I wasn't allowed to take them off. I knew why. My hair fell off every day and kids with lupus didn't need the sun. So I always wore my cap.

5

Granny and I

"Let's play, 'I COUNT'," Chichi said,

"No, it's too long. And you always win. How about 'Bree and the snow castle'!" I said,

"But there's no snow, and you will get tired," Chichi said,

We thought and thought searching for the perfect game.

"Where is my favorite granddaughter?!" said a familiar voice.

"Granny!" Chichi and I screamed as we raced to the living room and into Granny's arms. Granny gave us a squishy hug and kept rubbing our heads.

"Look how grown you are and so pretty. Oh God bless you, my babies." She said.

"Here are the treats I got for my only granddaughter and her beautiful friend!" Granny said.

We said thank you and ran off to enjoy our treats. There were some cool toys and lots of sweets.

Chichi begged her parents for a sleepover because Granny was fun to be with. She told us several stories from the bible and I always enjoyed them. I loved the story about a boy who beat the mean giant.

"God loves every one of us including you my babies, so you must learn to pray," Granny said.

"Granny, did God give me lupus?" I asked,

"Oh, my dear. God gives us only good things. But he loves you. When your body hurts or you feel weak, just remember that." She answered.

When it was time for bed, my parents tucked us in. And as we closed our eyes, I could hear their voices praying to God. I slept, and I dreamt of playing in a field of pretty roses. They smelled great.

Granny promised she would stay for a long time. I was happy because I got better. Dr. Chin called me a tough kid and told me I was doing well. I believed him because I wasn't so tired anymore.

I only remembered my lupus when I took my medications. But I still didn't have much hair. Mommy and Daddy were happy too. We went for more picnics now and I ran and played all the best games with Chichi. I chased butterflies too.

"Daddy, do other children have lupus?" I asked one day on our way from the store.

"Well, yes, Natalie. A lot of children have lupus too." He told me.

"That means they might be sad or have stiff fingers. Can we visit them?" I asked,

"Well... I don't know honey. We will ask Mommymy at home, okay?" he said.

I didn't let Daddydy forget. Mommymy said we could visit some kids with lupus. So, I told Chichi about my big visit and my plan to share happy cards. We worked hard after school making the cards ourselves. We drew lots of happy faces and Daddydy showed us some nice words to add. Chichi begged her parents again to let her come with me.

When it was time for the big visit, I put all the cards in my backpack. We went to Mommy's hospital, but I never knew it was so big. There were so many rooms on the other side of the hospital. A nurse came with us and she showed us which rooms to go to. Some of the kids came to see the doctor for their lupus check. So, we gave them our cards. Then we met a kid named Jacob who was very sick. Mommy didn't want me to see Jacob, she was mad at the nurse for bringing us there. But Chichi and I sneaked away from her as they spoke.

"Hi," I said.

"H… i," Jacob said, he was very tired.

"I brought you a happy card. Here," and I put it in his hands.

"Thank… you…" Jacob said.

"I have lupus too. Granny said to pray if we are in pain. Let's pray for you," I said, and we held his hands and told Jesus to take the pain away so Jacob could be better like me.

Chichi tried telling Jacob some fun stories from school. He smiled and looked happy. My Mommy stood by the door the entire time. She had tears in her eyes, but they were happy tears. I looked back and smiled at her once. Jacob couldn't talk for long, so Chichi and I did all the talking. It was fun. Then after a while, he suddenly started coughing. The nurse rushed in and my Mommy came to take us out. I looked back and waved at Jacob before we were gone.

That evening Granny said she was proud of us for making other kids smile today. Then she asked Chichi to say Grace for our meal.

"Dear Jesus, thank you for our food. Thank you for our mothers and fathers and granny. Bless them and bless our food. Thank you for Natalie because you will take her lupus away and we will all be happy. Amen," Chichi prayed.

"Amen," everyone said.

Every day was better for me. I was stronger and happier. But then it changed and started all over again, which made me sad. I couldn't get up in the morning. My head hurt. So did my mouth, my arms, and legs. I tried not to be a crybaby. I prayed a little in my heart. When Granny came into my room, she sat by my side and sang.

"She's burning up. We have to see Dr. Chin. Come on, baby." Mommy said and Daddydy helped carry me to the car. I stared at my room until I couldn't see it anymore. Then I slept.

6

The Angels and Jesus in Heaven.

I spent a very long time in the hospital. My Mommy and Daddy brought all my toys to the hospital. I played with them when I could or when Chichi came to visit.

I was very sick now like Jacob. I heard my parents talking to Dr. Chin about lupus getting worse. He said my organs didn't work properly anymore especially my kidney. Lupus made my kidney bad, and this made me very sick.

Mommy, Daddy, and granny took turns to stay with me. They always prayed for me and told me stories of Jesus' love. After a few weeks in the hospital, I remembered Jacob was just like me. I wanted to go visit him again.

"Mommy, can we visit Jacob?" I asked,

"Jacob… oh… Jacob isn't here anymore. I will ask the nurse okay?" my Mommy said,

"Okay" I said.

More days passed, and I wasn't better. One night, Mommy, Daddy, and granny stayed with me together. My cousin came too, and I was happy because I only saw him on holidays. I smiled, and he held my hands.

"My baby. I hope you feel good." Granny said,

I nodded and tried to speak even though it was so hard.

"Granny… what happens… when...we...die?" I asked,

"Well, baby, when someone dies their body stops working. Everyone who knew them will miss them because they won't be around anymore." Granny said,

"But you know something that never dies? It's love. Your love and our love is connected by an invisible string. And no matter what happens or where we go, it keeps us connected. So you can always feel this love." Granny continued.

"Jesus takes those who die to live with him in heaven. They are always happy." Mommy said.

"I love you," I said, and I smiled even more. I was very tired now. I wanted to sleep again. As I closed my eyes, I felt a lot of hugs and heard a beautiful song. When I woke up I was in heaven. Jesus held my hands, and I was happy. I didn't feel tired anymore. I felt safe and happy just like Granny and my Mommy said I would. I lived with the angels and played with them.

I knew I died and everyone would miss me now. But I kept the invisible string of love close to my heart and when I miss anyone, I just think of them. So, now you know how I got to heaven.

My friend Chichi misses me a lot. She sends letters in balloons up to heaven. She tells me many stories and how Berta the mean girl stopped being so mean. My family made a memory box, and they put some of my stuff in it. It was a cute box, and it had my pictures, favorite toy, my flute, and my cool socks too. It helped them think of me in their hearts.

What is Lupus?

Lupus is a disease that some children or adults can have. It happens when your immune system attacks your body. Although that is mean, it is also bad for your health. Not everyone can have lupus. There are kids and adults who can have lupus if something triggers the disease. This trigger could be an infection, drugs, or sunlight.

If you have lupus, here are some things you might feel or notice.

- Tired all the time like Natalie
- Rashes when you go out in the sun. Especially a butterfly-shaped rash on your cute face.
- Body pain, swollen joints, stiff fingers.
- Angry or sad all the time.
- Fever
- Hair loss
- Memory loss
- Ulcers in the mouth.

Some people notice different signs of lupus. And you might look very healthy too. Nobody knows what really causes lupus and nobody knows a cure either. The medications can always help you feel better, so you must take them at the right time every day.

Lupus is not contagious which means you can't give anyone else lupus. You can play and go to school like other kids.

It's not your fault when you have lupus. It's not anyone's fault. Just keep being you and you will be fine!

Things to do if you have lupus

- Always tell your teachers, parents or doctor how you feel. Don't be afraid or shy.
- Always wash your hands to avoid germs.
- Don't play or sit with anyone who is sick with cold or other contagious diseases. It is not good for you.
- Always wear clothes that protect your skin from the sun. This means long sleeves, pants, and caps. When you need to rest, find a shade to rest under.
- It's okay to tell your friends you have lupus. This way they understand if you have to miss school or skip some activities.
- Don't be afraid to ask your friends or teachers for help. Tell your teacher if you feel pain or tiredness.

Remember lupus can be tricky and just because you don't see it on the outside, doesn't mean it isn't there. It's like a stomachache you can't see. Lupus is what you feel.

If the doctor says you have lupus or someone you love has lupus, never forget that lupus does not define you. Remember to pray to Jesus and do your best cause people will always remember the way you made them feel, even after you leave to live with Jesus. Natalie was always smiling, which made everyone around her smile too.

My special message

"If you have a friend who has lupus, don't be afraid. Always pray to Jesus for them. Be a good friend like Chichi who always knew when I was too tired to play or stand in the sun. Be a good classmate who cares when a friend with lupus has to stay home or go to the hospital. You can even make cards as I did. If they die, they will be just like me, happy and safe in heaven. You can do a lot of things to remember them, like plant a garden they would like, or name your pet after them, or build a memory box. You can send letters too like Chichi. You can cry when you want because you miss them. They miss you too.

If you are just like me, then be the best kid ever with lupus. Spend all your days with your loved ones making sure everyone is happy and smiling.

My name is Natalie and I live in heaven with angels. On Earth, I was a unique kid with lupus. Now I live in Heaven and I'm able to run and play and sing and laugh forever and ever!"

Natalie, smiles.

About the Author:

Chiemeri is a Recording Artist, Theater Actress and Writer who resides in the Houston Texas Area. She has two children and a Bonus Baby through her relationship with her spouse. Natalie and Chiemeri were friends since she was 7 and Natalie was 4. Their friendship lasted decades until her untimely death where she went to be with The Lord after complications with Lupus. Natalie'sHospice Nurse gave Chiemeri comforting words, letting her know Natalie talked about her often, even up to her last day. Chiemeri and Natalie shared a special sisterly bond, and she finds comfort knowing Natalie loved The Lord so much, and will see her again in Heaven.

Made in the USA
Monee, IL
21 January 2021

56728608R00018